Calamity Jane

Tale retold by Larry Dane Brimner
Illustrated by Judy DuFour Love

Adviser: Dr. Alexa Sandmann, Professor of Literacy,
The University of Toledo; Member, International Reading Association

School Dist. 64
164 S. Prospect Ave.
Park Ridge, IL 60068

 COMPASS POINT BOOKS
Minneapolis, Minnesota

George Washington School
Learning Resource Center

Compass Point Books
3109 West 50th Street, #115
Minneapolis, MN 55410

Visit Compass Point Books on the Internet at *www.compasspointbooks.com*
or e-mail your request to *custserv@compasspointbooks.com*

Dedication
To kids everywhere who march to the beat of different drummers.
  -LDB

Photographs ©: Bettmann/Corbis, 30; Corbis, 31.

Editor: Catherine Neitge
Photo Researcher: Svetlana Zhurkina
Designer: Les Tranby

Library of Congress Cataloging-in-Publication Data
The cataloging-in-publication data is on file with the Library of Congress.
ISBN 0-7565-0600-X
          2003019507

Table of Contents

In a Calamity

The soldiers dug in their spurs, urging their horses farther across the Wyoming plain. Whirling up around them, dust blocked the sun. Martha Jane Cannary pulled a kerchief around her nose and mouth. Even so, it brought little relief from the thick dust. It burned her throat and stung her eyes. She was lucky to be able to see the soldier and horse in front of her. She could hear only the thundering sound of hooves.

The West was a wild place in those days. Only the folks who inhabited it were wilder. Although

some in those parts may tell a different story—and they would most likely be right—it was the United States Army that tried to tame the West. Martha Jane was part of that Army. She was the first woman to serve that dignified group in uniform—if history is told right, and often it isn't. She could outride, outshoot, and outboast any soldier the Army dared put up against her. She was the most courageous soldier ever to ride a horse into battle, and she was the boldest. She would tell you so herself, if given the chance. It would all be facts, too, unless it was fiction.

One of Martha Jane's boldest adventures happened one day on a dusty plain in Wyoming. A rowdy gang of ruffians was acting up against the miners who were trying their best to scratch out enough gold from that area to call it an honest living. The ruffians were the wildest, meanest, fiercest, most toothless cusses in those parts. They liked gold. They didn't care much for mining or miners. Work, after all, wasn't for the likes of them. Martha Jane and her fellow soldiers had been ordered to chase off the good-for-nothings so the miners could get back to their mines.

Hooves pounded the earth. Dust and dirt flew up all around the soldiers.

Crack! Suddenly, there was a rifle shot, then more.

The skirmish was fierce, with fighting all around. Soldiers tangled with varmints. Varmints tangled with soldiers. Martha Jane took two of the galoots by surprise, letting out a *whoop-ee-i-i-ee!* It so startled the ruffians that they were knocked clean out of their saddles! They hightailed it on foot lickety-split to Canada and never once looked back. Martha Jane barely mussed her long, red hair.

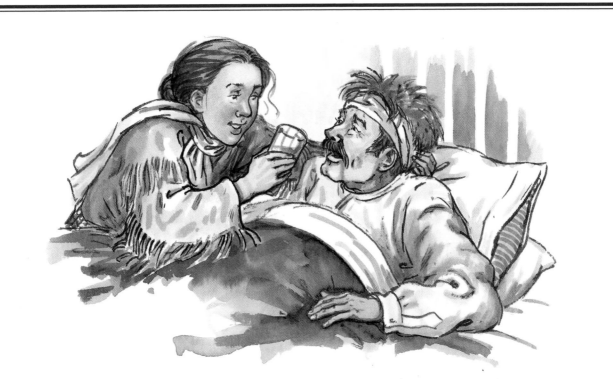

Crack! Another shot sounded.

Martha Jane looked in the direction of the shot. "Captain Egan!" she shouted. The captain was down. His horse had run off to safer ground.

Martha Jane lost no time. In a blink, she spurred her horse and galloped straight toward the captain—and danger.

The ruffian, who had plans of his own for the captain, never saw her coming. In one smooth motion, Martha Jane unseated the varmint, scooped up the captain, pitched

him across her horse, and rode off to safety.

The varmint? He pitched a fit before hotfooting it to parts unknown and was never heard from again.

Later that afternoon, Martha Jane tended the captain's wound. "Martha Jane," he said, "you're pretty handy to have around in a calamity. From this moment forward, I name you Calamity Jane, the heroine of the plains."

That's how Martha Jane came to be Calamity Jane.

Fearless

Martha Jane was an unusual child, as you might guess. (Legends usually are, you know!) When the stork delivered her to Princeton, Missouri, in 1852, it didn't bother dropping her into a cradle. Oh, no. It set her down atop a horse, and Martha Jane rode from that day forward. She took to horses the way a fish takes to water. Why, she became such an expert rider that by the age of 3 she was taming the wildest of the beasts.

By the time she set out with her family for Montana, she was also a crack shot with her pa's rifle. To hear her tell it, she could pick a pheasant out of a field blindfolded while standing on her head. It's a good thing, too. During that five-month journey, her family and the other pioneers in the wagon train

sometimes ran out of food. Martha Jane always came through, though. She'd gallop her horse right alongside the men in the hunting party. Then before the men could even take aim with their rifles, Martha Jane had dinner ready to cook.

The journey wasn't all riding and hunting, of course. When the pioneers were fording streams with their wagons, sometimes Martha Jane swam back and forth just for fun. One time, however, the raging river swept her quickly away. Everyone in the wagon train feared the worst when, suddenly, a half-mile downstream, Martha Jane popped out of the water.

"That was refreshing," she announced to the party searching for her. "Anyone care to join me?" There were no takers, so she jumped in again and swam back upstream in time to help the last wagon cross.

That Martha Jane! She was fearless.

Take the time the family's wagon train met up with a band of Native Americans. The Indians didn't take kindly to pioneers coming to settle their land. The United States government had given it to the Indians, after all, in exchange for other land it had taken from them. It was theirs by treaty. Of course, as soon as gold was discovered, the government whistled a different tune. It wanted the Native Americans to pack up and move again. The government told the pioneers the land could now be theirs. Governments are like that sometimes, but the Indians didn't like it. Can you imagine that?

So, the band of Indians circled the wagons. The pioneers didn't know what to expect. Could it be the end?

It wasn't the end, though—no, not by a long shot. Martha Jane jumped on her horse and rode out to face the Native Americans. Of course, she did it in her own way— balanced on her head.

The Indians had never seen such a sight. As quick as a cricket can hop, they decided the young rider was a bad omen. They thought it best not to tangle with these pioneers—at least not as long as this strange, red-haired apparition was among them.

Word spread after that. From that day forward, Martha Jane could ride among any of the Native Americans and receive the greatest respect—and distance.

Frontier Scout

By the time Martha Jane became Calamity Jane, she knew the frontier as well as a calf knows its mother. The United States Army asked her to be a scout. That sounded better than doing laundry or cooking, so she agreed to do it.

It was while scouting for the Army that Calamity was ordered to join up with General George Armstrong Custer. That was in 1876. Between courting fame and posing for pictures, the general was marching to the Montana Territory. He was charged with driving out the Indians, many of whom were camped on the banks of the Little Bighorn River.

19

Fate must have been looking out for Calamity because she never made it to the Little Bighorn on that trip. Along the way, she forded the Platte River. Dripping wet, freezing cold, and trying to put more trail behind her than was ahead of her, she got pneumonia. She was taken back to camp and kept in the hospital for 14 days. As it turned out, getting pneumonia was a lucky mishap. The general and his troops were killed right there on the banks of the Little Bighorn River. Today, we call the bloody battle Custer's Last Stand, and so it was. He and all the soldiers with him died.

When Calamity was able to ride again, luck smiled on her once more in the form of one Wild Bill Hickok. A famous lawman, Wild Bill was as dashing as Calamity was daring. The two were meant for each other, and to hear some folks tell it, that's just the way it was. Together, they set out for the town of Deadwood, South Dakota. The pair was as happy as a snail in its shell . . . for a while.

Then misfortune struck. While sitting at a gambling table, Wild Bill was shot dead by Jack McCall, a notorious outlaw. On hearing the news, Calamity hunted down the no-good killer and single-handedly brought him to justice.

Only a fool would dare tangle with Calamity Jane!

Special Delivery

Through the years, Calamity held a number of jobs. She delivered mail and money between Deadwood and Custer, South Dakota. It was one of the most rugged trails in the West and thick with thieves. The toll collectors (that's Old West talk for robbers) left Calamity alone, though. They knew she was an expert shot and didn't want to take any chances. Even so, she still had adventures.

Take the morning she saw a stagecoach at some distance bringing more settlers to the area. The horses were galloping at a full run, and the driver was keeled over in the seat. A gang of toll collectors chased behind it. Calamity spurred her horse, Satan, into action and finally caught up with the coach. She urged Satan on, standing astride his back. When, at last, she was close enough, she leapt upon the lead horse and brought the stage safely to a stop.

The toll collectors? As soon as they saw it was Calamity saving the stagecoach from certain disaster, they hightailed it in the opposite direction.

Calamity held down many jobs and had many adventures throughout the Wild West, but she always returned to the Black Hills. Before she died, she made one last request: "Bury me next to Wild Bill, ya hear?" Friends saw to it that she was.

The Life of Calamity Jane

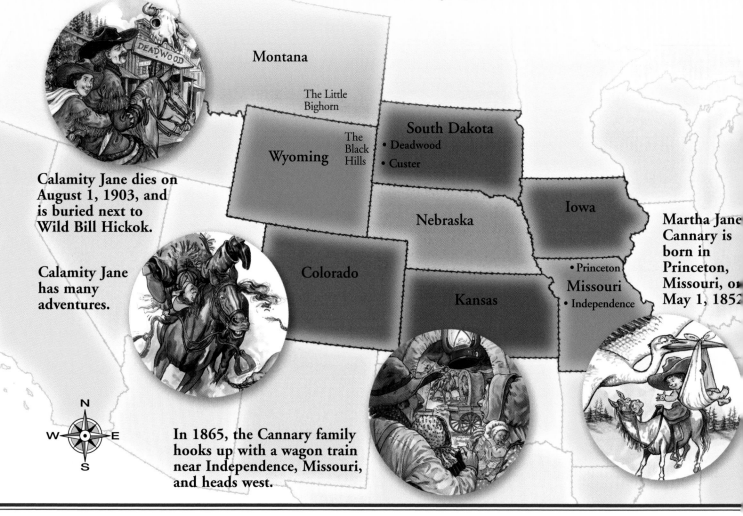

Montana

The Little Bighorn

Wyoming

The Black Hills

South Dakota
• Deadwood
• Custer

Iowa

Nebraska

Colorado

Kansas

Missouri
• Princeton
• Independence

Martha Jane Cannary is born in Princeton, Missouri, on May 1, 1852.

Calamity Jane dies on August 1, 1903, and is buried next to Wild Bill Hickok.

Calamity Jane has many adventures.

In 1865, the Cannary family hooks up with a wagon train near Independence, Missouri, and heads west.

Calamity Jane was a real person, and it was she who started telling many of the stories about her adventures. Her legend grew when a writer named Edward Lytton Wheeler paired a character he called Calamity Jane with Deadwood Dick in a series of dime novels in the late 1800s. The books were so popular that people started confusing the lives of Wheeler's Calamity Jane and the real Calamity Jane. Even Calamity seemed to confuse her own real-life adventures with those invented by Wheeler. Years later, it is hard for historians to sort out the truth from the fiction.

We do know this: Calamity Jane was probably an Army scout, a nurse, a cook, a prospector, and a gambler. It is also true that she was a sharpshooter who could drink and cuss as well as any soldier. She wore pants and even chewed tobacco. But was she close to Wild Bill Hickok? Did she ever deliver the mail? Did she ever know Captain Egan, much less save his life? Historians don't really know.

The other truth about Calamity Jane is that she gave America a glimpse of a liberated woman in a time when most women did not have many choices in life. Her spirit of independence, strength, and pride is what lives in the many legends of Calamity Jane.

Honey-Mustard Barbecue Sandwiches

On the trail, pioneers usually made do with whatever wild animals they caught, and they cooked up the meat over an open fire. They would have loved this sandwich and the ease with which it is made! It serves six hungry pioneers.

1 medium onion, cut in quarters
3 whole cloves garlic, peeled
2-to-3 pounds boneless beef chuck roast, cut into three or four chunks
1 teaspoon salt

1/2 teaspoon black pepper
3/4 cup water
1 cup bottled honey-mustard barbecue sauce
6 hamburger buns or kaiser rolls, split
chopped green bell pepper and/or onion

Place the onion and garlic in a slow cooker. Add the beef chunks, then the salt, pepper, and water. Cover and cook on low for 9 hours, or until beef shreds apart with a fork. Remove the beef from the cooking liquid, saving and straining the liquid. Allow the beef to cool slightly. Then shred the beef with forks.

In a 1 1/2-quart microwave-safe dish, combine the shredded beef, 1/4-cup of reserved cooking liquid, and the barbecue sauce. Mix thoroughly. Cover and microwave on high for 5 to 6 minutes, or until hot. Spoon equal amounts of the beef over the bottom half of each bun. Sprinkle with chopped green pepper and/or onion. Top with the other half of the bun. Enjoy right away.

Glossary

apparition—something seen; a vision

dime novels—popular reading material in the late 1800s (called "dime" novels even though they sometimes cost only a nickel!)

fording—crossing a river where it is shallow

galoots—foolish or silly people

inhabited—lived in

liberated—someone not bound by tradition or rules

notorious—widely known for something bad

omen—sign of an event to come

ruffians—bullies

skirmish—small battle

varmints—pests or bullies

The real Calamity Jane posed for a studio photograph in the 1880s.

Did You Know?

➤ Calamity Jane starred in old-time Wild West shows. She showed off her sharpshooting skills by shooting silver dollars and entertained the audiences with tales of her adventures.

➤ Another job Calamity Jane had was bullwhacker—driving teams of oxen pulling heavy wagons. Calamity claimed she could use a whip so well that she could pick a fly off an ox's ear "four times out of five."

➤ Even though it is part of her legend, there is no evidence to prove that Calamity Jane ever scouted for General George Armstrong Custer.

➤ Calamity Jane and Wild Bill Hickok probably knew each other, but their story likely ends there. Wild Bill was happily married to someone else when he met Calamity Jane. His wife owned a circus.

➤ It is said that Calamity's heart was as big as her legend. When smallpox hit the Black Hills in 1878, she nursed sick miners around the clock—feeding them, bathing them, and burying them if they didn't survive.

Want to Know More?

At the Library

Burke, Martha Cannary. *Life and Adventures of Calamity Jane by Herself.* Fairfield, Wash.: Ye Galleon Press, 1979.

Faber, Doris. *Calamity Jane: Her Life and Her Legend.* Boston: Houghton Mifflin Company, 1992.

Sanford, William R., and Carl R. Green. *Calamity Jane: Frontier Original.* Berkeley Heights, N.J.: Enslow Publishers, Inc., 1996.

Spies, Karen. *Our Folk Heroes.* Brookfield, Conn.: The Millbrook Press, 1994.

On the Web

For more information on *Calamity Jane,* use FactHound to track down Web sites related to this book.

1. Go to *www.compasspointbooks.com/ facthound*
2. Type in this book ID: 075650600X
3. Click on the *Fetch It* button.

Your trusty FactHound will fetch the best Web sites for you!

Through the Mail

Deadwood Chamber of Commerce and Visitors Bureau
735 Main St.
Deadwood, SD 57732
800/999-1876
visit@deadwood.org
To write for information on historic Deadwood, where the real Calamity Jane lived and died

On the Road

Moriah Cemetery
Deadwood, SD 57732
To see where Calamity Jane and Wild Bill Hickok are buried

Calamity Jane stands next to Wild Bill Hickok's grave in Deadwood in July 1903. She died the following month and was buried there, too.

Index

About the Author

Larry Dane Brimner has written more than 100 books for young people, including the award-winning *Merry Christmas, Old Armadillo* (Boyds Mills Press) and *The Littlest Wolf* (HarperCollins Publishers). He is also the reteller of several other Tall Tales, including *Captain Stormalong, Casey Jones, Davy Crockett,* and *Molly Pitcher*. Mr. Brimner lives in historic Old Pueblo (Tucson, Arizona).

About the Illustrator

Judy DuFour Love received a Bachelor of Fine Arts degree from the Rhode Island School of Design. She lives near Boston, Massachusetts, with her two sons, Matt and Tom, and two cats, Jeremy and Fluffy. She has always loved drawing, especially creating imagery to accompany stories.

School Dist. 64
164 S. Prospect Ave.
Park Ridge, IL 60068